W9-AGG-089

The Puddle Pail

ELISA KLEVEN

DUTTON CHILDREN'S BOOKS · NEW YORK

Library of Congress Cataloging-in-Publication Data

Kleven, Elisa.
The puddle pail / by Elisa Kleven. — 1st ed.
p.   cm.
Summary: When his older green brother suggests that he collect
things, Ernst, a young blue crocodile, comes up with an
unusual choice: puddles.
ISBN 0-525-45803-4
[1. Brothers — Fiction.   2. Crocodiles — Fiction.
3. Collectors and collecting — Fiction.]   I. Title.
PZ7.K6783875Pu   1997   [E] — dc21   96-45291   CIP   AC

Published in the United States 1997 by
Dutton Children's Books, a division of Penguin Books USA Inc.
375 Hudson Street, New York, New York 10014

Designed by Sara Reynolds
Printed in Hong Kong
First Edition
1   3   5   7   9   10   8   6   4   2

One bright morning after a storm, Ernst, a young blue crocodile, and his big green brother, Sol, set off for the beach. They skipped through the wet grass and stamped through the mud, drumming on their shiny pails.

"I'm going to fill my pail with shells," said Sol, who loved to collect things.

"I'm going to fill my pail with sand and build a sand castle," said Ernst, who loved to make things.

"Maybe I'll find some rocks, too," said Sol, "all shapes and colors, for my rock collection. And some feathers, for my feather collection, and maybe some string." Sol bent down to pick up a rubber band. "Just the thing for my rubber band collection! You ought to start a collection, Ernst."

"I don't know what to collect," Ernst replied.

"Collect something you really like," said Sol. "Something that comes in all different sizes and colors and shapes. That way your collection will be interesting."

Ernst watched the clouds make flower shapes and sea horse shapes in the windy sky. He watched a little snake-cloud puff up into a dragon. He watched a rabbit cloud curl into a ball.

"Clouds are interesting," he said. "I wish I could collect clouds."

"Clouds!" exclaimed Sol. "You can't collect clouds! Think of something else you like."

"Stars," said Ernst, imagining the sky at night. "I love to watch the stars."

"But you can't collect stars, either," said Sol. "They're too far away and too big and very, very hot."

"They look so small and cold," said Ernst. "I wish I could collect stars."

"I know!" said Sol. "Starfishes! You could collect *them.*"

"I like starfishes in the ocean," said Ernst. "But I don't think I want to collect them."

"Well," Sol suggested, "what about star-shaped cookies? You could collect star-shaped butter cookies with frosting—"

"And star-shaped chocolate cookies with sprinkles," Ernst added.

"And star-shaped cherry cookies with toasted nuts!" said Sol.

Ernst's mouth watered. "I wish I could collect a bunch of cookies right now—in my stomach!"

Just then, something caught Sol's eye—a bottle cap lying in a puddle. "Look at that sparkly bottle cap, Ernst. You could start a bottle cap collection!"

"It's pretty," Ernst agreed. "But I like the puddle it's in even more."

"The puddle?" said Sol.

"It looks like a little piece of sky on the ground. I wish I could collect *it*."

"You can't collect puddles," said Sol.

"Yes, I can collect puddles," said Ernst. "They're not too far away or too big or too hot—and I don't want to eat them." *Splish-splash*, Ernst scooped the puddle into his pail.

"Ernst," said Sol, "you're not really going to start a puddle collection, are you?"

"Yes," said Ernst, "I am." He scooped up a green puddle, round as a saucer. *Splash-splosh*, it joined the other puddle in the pail.

Sol rolled his eyes. "Since you're going to stay here collecting puddles, I'll go down to the beach by myself and collect *real* things."

Puddles are real, thought Ernst, as he searched for more to collect. "Here's a purple puddle...

and a striped one

and a flowered one.

Here's a puddle full of diamonds and a puddle full of squares...

a puddle full of gumballs and a puddle full of brooms,

a puddle like an Easter egg,

a puddle like a wheel and a puddle with a pretzel in it.

Slippery puddles, smooth puddles, lemony, lettery cool puddles."
Ernst sang a song as he scooped the puddles up. *Splish-splash* sang
the puddles as they slid into the pail.

Sol came back with his pail piled high. "Look what I got, Ernst!
Twelve seashells,

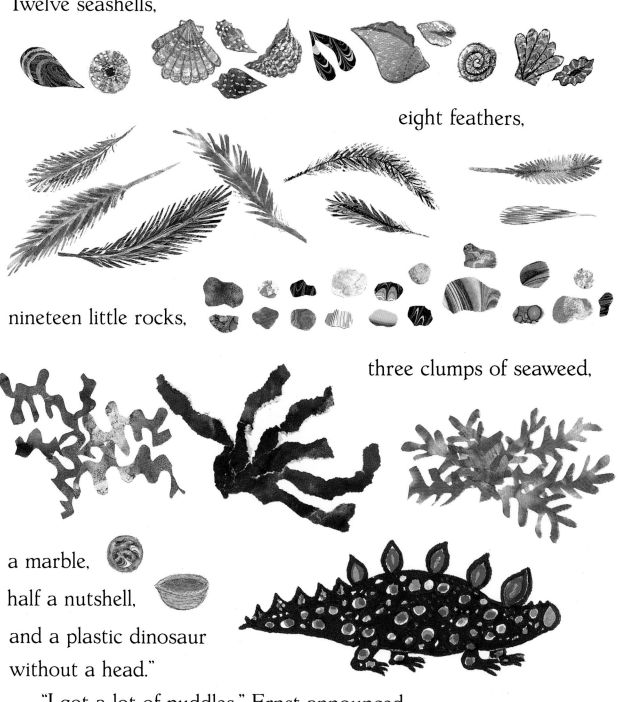

eight feathers,

nineteen little rocks,

three clumps of seaweed,

a marble,
half a nutshell,
and a plastic dinosaur
without a head."

"I got a lot of puddles," Ernst announced.
"All different sizes and colors and shapes."

Sol peered into Ernst's pail. "Your puddles have all run together! They look like a pail full of ordinary water!"

"They're one *big* puddle now," said Ernst. "An Ernst and Sol puddle!"

"That's the weirdest collection I've ever heard of," Sol replied. "What can you do with a puddle?"

"I'll think of something." Ernst carried his pail carefully as they started for home.

"I know!" said Sol. "You can help me wash the sand off all my new collections."

"You can wash your own collections," Ernst replied. "I'll think of something else to do with my puddle."

Ernst set his puddle pail on the grass and sat down to swing.
While he swung, his puddle slowly turned from gold to pink.
Clouds swam in and out of it like fishes.

When night fell, stars collected in the puddle pail—and a little piece of the moon, too.

Early the next morning, Ernst went out to check on his pail. A thirsty dog was drinking from it. "You like my magic puddle soup?" Ernst asked. The dog wagged her tail and drank some more, leaving Ernst just enough water to paint some watercolor pictures.

Ernst painted the dog,

and he painted some clouds

and some stars and many puddles.

Sol came by, his pail filled with flowers and acorns and leaves. "I started some new collections," he said. "What have you got there, Ernst?"

"A dog," replied Ernst. "And a painting collection."

"Oooh!" said Sol. "What a collection! With clouds and stars and everything."

"I used part of my puddle collection to make it," Ernst explained. "The dog drank the other part."

Ernst petted the dog. He looked at the clouds and the stars and the puddles, shining on the grass. He felt proud and happy—and hungry, too, since he hadn't eaten breakfast yet.

"Let's go collect blackberries," he said, "from the bushes down the road."

"Good idea!" Sol grabbed his pail. "Maybe we'll find some pennies on the way, and some pinecones and gum wrappers."

"And maybe some shadows, too," said Ernst.

"Shadows!" said Sol. "You can't—"

"Yes, I can collect shadows!" Ernst cried. He caught one for a second in his pail.

And when it fluttered off, he and Sol filled their pails—and themselves—with sweet, juicy blackberries.